CHARLOTTE BRONTË

MINA LAURY

PENGUIN BOOKS

PENGUIN BOOKS

Published by the Penguin Group
Penguin Books Ltd, 27 Wrights Lane, London W8 5TZ, England
Penguin Books USA Inc., 375 Hudson Street, New York, New York 10014, USA
Penguin Books Australia Ltd, Ringwood, Victoria, Australia
Penguin Books Canada Ltd, 10 Alcorn Avenue, Toronto, Ontario, Canada M4V 3B2
Penguin Books (NZ) Ltd, 182–190 Wairau Road, Auckland 10, New Zealand

Penguin Books Ltd, Registered Offices: Harmondsworth, Middlesex, England

This selection is from *The Juvenilia of Jane Austen and Charlotte Brontë*,
edited by Frances Beer, published in Penguin Classics 1986
This edition published 1995
1 3 5 7 9 10 8 6 4 2

Printed in England by Clays Ltd, St Ives plc

The Cross of Rivaulx! Is that a name familiar to my readers? I rather think not. Listen then: it is a green, delightful, and quiet place half way between Angria and the foot of the Sydenham Hills; under the frown of Hawkscliffe, on the edge of its royal forest. You see a fair house, whose sash windows are set in ivy grown thick and kept in trim order; over the front door there is a little modern porch of trellis work, all the summer covered with a succession of verdant leaves and pink rose-globes, buds and full-blown blossoms. Within this, in fine weather, the door is constantly open and reveals a noble passage, almost a hall, terminating in a staircase of low white steps, traced up the middle by a brilliant carpet. You look in vain for anything like a wall or gate to shut it in: the only landmark consists in an old obelisk with moss and wild flowers at its base and an half obliterated crucifix sculptured on its side.

Well, this is no very presuming place, but on a June

evening not seldom have I seen a figure, whom every eye in Angria might recognise, stride out of the domestic gloom of that little hall and stand in pleasant leisure under the porch whose flowers and leaves were disturbed by the contact of his curls. Though in a sequestered spot, the Cross of Rivaulx is not one of Zamorna's secret houses; he'll let anybody come there that chooses.

The day is breathless, quite still and warm. The sun, far declined for afternoon, is just melting into evening, and sheds a deep amber light. A cheerful air surrounds the mansion whose windows are up, its door as usual hospitably apart, and the broad passage reverberates with a lively conversational hum from the rooms which open into it. The day is of that perfectly mild, sunny kind that by an irresistible influence draws people out into the balmy air; see, there are two gentlemen lounging easily in the porch, sipping coffee from the cups they have brought from the drawing room; a third has stretched himself on the soft moss in the shadow of the obelisk. But for these figures, the landscape could be one of exquisite repose.

Two, [in military dress], are officers from the headquarters of Zamorna's grand army; the other, reclining on the grass, a slight figure in black, wears a civil dress. That is Mr Warner, the home secretary. Another person was standing by him whom I should not have omitted to describe. It was a fine girl, dressed in rich black satin, with ornaments like those of a bandit's wife in which a whole fortune seemed to have been expended; but no wonder, for they had doubtless been the gift of a king. In her ears hung two long clear drops, red as fire, and suffused with a purple tint that showed them to be the true oriental ruby. Bright delicate links of gold circled her neck again and again, and a cross of gems lay on her breast, the centre stone of which was a locket enclosing a ringlet of dark brown hair—with that little soft curl she would not have parted for a kingdom.

Warner's eyes were fixed with interest on Miss Laury as she stood over him, a model of beautiful vigour and glowing health; there was a kind of military erectness in her form, so elegantly built, and in the manner in which her neck, sprung from her exquisite bust, was placed with graceful uprightness on her falling shoulders. Her waits too, falling in behind, and her fine slender foot, supporting her in a regulated position, plainly indicated familiarity from her childhood with the sergeant's drill. All the afternoon she had been entertaining her exalted guests—the two in the porch were no other than Lord Hartford and Enara—and conversing with them, frankly and cheerfully. These were the only friends she had in the world. Female acquaintance she never sought, nor if she had sought, would she have found them. And so sagacious, clever, and earnest was she in all she said and did, that the haughty aristocrats did not hesitate to communicate with her often on matters of first-rate importance.

Mr Warner was now talking to her about herself.

'My dear madam,' he was saying in his usual imperious and still dulcet tone, 'it is unreasonable that you should remain this exposed to danger. I am your friend—yes, madam, your *true* friend. Why do you not hear me and attend to my representations of the case? Angria is an unsafe place for you. You ought to leave it.' The lady shook her head.

'Never. Till my master compels me, his land is my land.'

'But—but, Miss Laury, you know that our army have no warrant from the Almighty. This invasion may be successful at least for a time; and then what becomes of you? When the duke's nation is wrestling

4

with destruction, his glory sunk in deep waters, and himself striving desperately to recover it, can he waste a thought or a moment on one woman?'

Mina smiled.

'I am resolved,' said she. 'My master himself shall not force me to leave him. You know I am hardened, Warner; shame and reproach have no effect on me. I do not care for being called a camp follower. In peace and pleasure all the ladies of Africa would be at the duke's beck; in war and suffering he shall not lack one poor peasant girl. Why, sir, I've nothing else to exist for. I've no other interest in life. Just to stand by his grace, watch him and anticipate his wishes, or when I cannot do that, to execute them like lightning when they are signified; to wait on him when he is sick or wounded, to hear his groans and bear his heart-rending animal patience in enduring pain; to breathe if I can my own inexhaustible health and energy into him, and oh, if it were practicable, to take his fever and agony; to guard his interests, to take on my shoulders power from him that galls me with its weight; to fill a gap in his mighty train of service which nobody else would dare to step into: to do all that, sir, is to fulfil the destiny I was born to. I know I am of no repute amongst society at large because I have devoted myself so wholly to one man. And I know that he even seldom troubles himself to think of what I do, has never and can never appreciate the unusual feelings of subservience, the total self-sacrifice I offer at his shrine. But then he gives me my reward, and that an abundant one.

'Mr Warner, when I was at Fort Adrian and had all the yoke of governing the garrison and military household, I used to rejoice in my responsibility, and to feel firmer, the heavier the weight assigned me to support. When my master came over, as he often did to take one of his general surveys, or on a hunting expedition with some of his state officers, I had such delight in ordering the banquets and entertainments, and in seeing the fires kindled up and the chandeliers lighted in those dark halls, knowing for whom the feast was made ready. It gave me a feeling of ecstasy to hear my young master's voice, to see him moving about secure and powerful in his own stronghold, to know what true hearts he had about him. Besides, sir, his greeting to me, and the condescending touch of his hand, were enough to make a queen proud, let alone a sergeant's daughter.

'Then, for instance, the last summer evening that he came here, the sun and flowers and quietness brightened his noble features with such happiness, I could tell his heart was at rest; for as he lay in the shade where you are now, I heard him hum the airs he long, long ago played on his guitar. I was rewarded then to feel that the house I kept was pleasant enough to make him forget Angria and recur to home. You must excuse me, Mr Warner, but the west, the sweet west, is both his home and mine.' Mina paused and looked solemnly at the sun, now softened in its shine and hanging exceedingly low. In a moment her eyes fell again on Warner. They seemed to have absorbed radiance from what they had gazed on: light like an arrow point glanced in them as she said,

'This is my time to follow Zamorna. I'll not be robbed of those hours of blissful danger when I may be continually with him. I am not afraid of danger; I have strong nerves; I will die or be with him.'

'What has fired your eyes so suddenly, Miss Laury?' asked Lord Hartford, now advancing with Enara from their canopy of roses.

'The duke, the duke,' muttered Enara. 'You won't leave him, I'll be sworn.'

'I can't, general,' said Mina.

'No,' answered the Italian, 'and nobody shall force you. You shall have your own way, madam, whether it be right or wrong. I hate to contradict such as you in their will.'

'Thank you, general, you are always so kind to me.' Mina hurriedly put her little hand into the gloved grasp of Enara.

'Kind, madam?' said he, pressing it warmly, 'I'm so kind that I would hang the man unshriven who should use your name with other than respect due to a queen.' The dark, hard-browed Hartford smiled at his enthusiasm.

'Is that homage paid to Miss Laury's goodness or to her beauty?' asked he.

'To neither, my lord,' answered Enara briefly, 'but to her worth, her sterling worth.'

'Hartford, you are not going to despise me? Was that a sneer?' murmured Mina aside.

'No. No, Miss Laury,' replied the noble general seriously. 'I know what you are; I am aware of your value. Do you doubt Edward Hartford's honourable friendship? It is yours on terms such as it was never given to a beautiful woman before.'

Before Miss Laury could answer, a voice from within the mansion spoke her name.

'It is my lord!' she exclaimed, and sped like a roe over the sward, through the porch, along the passage, to a summer parlour, whose walls were painted fine pale red, its mouldings burnished gilding, and its window curtains artistical draperies of dark blue silk, covered with gold waves and flowers.

Here Zamorna sat alone; he had been writing. One or two letters, folded, sealed, and inscribed with western directions lay on the table beside him. He had not uncovered since entering the house three hours since, and either the weight of his dragoon helmet, or the gloom of its impending plumes, or else some inward feeling, had clouded his face with a strange darkness.

Mina closed the door and softly drew near; without speaking or asking leave, she began to busy herself in unclasping the heavy helmet. The duke smiled faintly as her little fingers played about his chin and luxuriant whiskers; and then, the load of brass and sable plumage being removed, as they arranged the compressed masses of glossy brown ringlets, and touched with soft cool contact his feverish brow. Absorbed in this grateful task she hardly felt that his majesty's arm had encircled her waist; yet she did feel it, too, and would have thought herself presumptuous to shrink from his endearment. She took it as a slave ought to take the caress of a sultan, and obeying the gentle effort of his hand, slowly sunk on to the sofa by her master's side.

'My little physician,' said he, meeting her adoring but anxious upward gaze with the full light of his countenance, 'you look at me as if you thought I was not well—feel my pulse.' She folded the proferred hand, white, supple, and soft with youth and delicate nurture, in both her own; whether Zamorna's pulse beat rapidly or not, his handmaid's did as she felt the slender grasping fingers of the monarch laid quietly in hers.

He did not wait for the report, but took his hand away again, and laying it on her raven curls said, 'So, Mina, you won't leave me, though I never did you any good in the world. Warner says you are resolved to continue in the scene of war.'

'To continue by your side, my lord duke.'

'But what shall I do with you, Mina? Where shall I put you? My little girl, what will the army say when they hear of your presence? You have read history; recollect that it was Darius who carried his concubines to the field, not Alexander. The world will say Zamorna has provided himself with a pretty mistress. He attends to his own pleasures and cares not how his men suffer.'

Poor Mina writhed at these words as if the iron had entered into her soul. A vivid burning blush crimsoned her cheek, and tears of shame and bitter self-reproach gushed at once into her bright black eyes. Zamorna was touched acutely.

'Nay, my little girl,' said he, redoubling his haughty caresses and speaking in his most soothing tone, 'never weep about it. It grieves me to hurt your feelings, but you desire an impossibility and I must use strong language to convince you that I cannot grant it—'

'Oh! don't refuse me again,' sobbed Miss Laury. 'I'll bear all infamy and contempt to be allowed to follow you, my lord. My lord, I've served you for many years most faithfully and I seldom ask a favour of you. Don't reject almost the first request of the kind I ever made.' The duke shook his head, and the meeting of his exquisite lips, too placid for the term compression, told he was not to be moved.

'If you should receive a wound, if you should fall sick,' continued Mina, 'what can surgeons and physicians do for you? They cannot watch you and wait on

11

you and worship you like me; you do not seem well now, the bloom is so faded on your complexion and the flesh is wasted round your eyes. My lord, smile and do not look so calmly resolved. Let me go!'

Zamorna withdrew his arm from her waist. 'I must be displeased before you cease to importune me,' said he. 'Mina, look at that letter, read the direction,' pointing to one he had been writing. She obeyed: it was addressed to Her Royal Highness Mary Henrietta, Duchess of Zamorna, Queen of Angria.

'Must I pay no attention to the feelings of that lady?' pursued the duke, whom the duties of war and the conflict of some internal emotions seemed to render rather peculiarly stern. 'Her public claims must be respected whether I love her or not.' Miss Laury shrunk into herself. Not another word did she venture to breathe. An unconscious wish of wild intensity filled her that she were dead and buried, insensible to the shame that overwhelmed her. She saw Zamorna's finger with the ring on it still pointing to that awful name, a name that raised no impulse of hatred, but only bitter humiliation and self-abasement. She stole from her master's side, feeling that she had no more right to sit there than a fawn has to share the den of a royal lion; and murmuring that she was very sorry for her folly, was about to glide in dismay and despair from the room. But the duke, rising up, arrested her, and bending his lofty stature over as she crouched before him, folded her again in his arms. His countenance relaxed not a moment from its sternness, nor did the gloom leave his magnificent but worn features, as he said,

'I will make no apologies for what I have said because I know, Mina, that, as I hold you now, you feel fully recompensed for my transient severity. Before I depart, I will speak to you one word of comfort, which you may remember when I am far away, and perhaps dead. My dear girl! I know and appreciate all you have done, all you have resigned, and all you have endured for my sake. I repay you for it with one coin, with what alone will be to you of greater worth than worlds without it. I give you such true and fond love as a master may give to the fairest and loveliest vassal that ever was bound to him in feudal allegiance. You may never feel the touch of Zamorna's lips again. There, Mina.' And fervently, almost fiercely, he pressed them to her forehead. 'Go to your chamber. Tomorrow you must leave for the west.'

13

'Obedient till death,' was Miss Laury's answer, as she closed the door and disappeared.

[Meanwhile ... though Zamorna has apparently directed a letter to his wife in this past scene, he persists in his decision to repudiate her and get revenge on her father, Northangerland, by breaking her heart. Weeks pass without a word from Zamorna, and Mary begins to pine away.]

The duchess dropped her head on her hand.

'Is the sun shining hot this evening?' said she. 'I feel very languid and inert.' Alas, it was not the mild sun of April glistening even now on the lingering rain drops of the morning which caused that sickly languor. 'I wish the mail would come in,' continued the duchess. 'How long is it since I've had a letter now, Amelia?'

'Three weeks, my lady.'

'If none comes this evening, what shall I do, Amelia? I shall never get on till tomorrow. Oh, I dread those long, weary, sleepless nights I've had lately, tossing through many hours on a wide, lonely bed, with the lamps decaying round me. Now I think I could sleep if I only had a kind letter for a talisman to press to my heart all night long. Amelia, I'd give anything to get from the east this evening a square of white paper directed in that light, rapid hand. Would he but write two lines to me signed with his name.'

'My lady,' said Miss Clifton, as she placed a little silver vessel of tea and a plate of biscuit before her mistress, 'you will hear from the east this evening, and that before many minutes elapse. Mr Warner is in Verdopolis and will wait upon you immediately.' It was pleasant to see how a sudden beam of joy shot into the settled sadness of Queen Mary's face.

'I am thankful to heaven for it,' exclaimed she. 'Even if he brings bad news it will be a relief from suspense; and if good news, this heart sickness will be removed for a moment.'

As she spoke, a foot was heard in the antechamber, there was a light tap at the door. Mr Warner entered closely muffled, as it was absolutely necessary that he should avoid remark, for the sacrifice of his liberty would have been the result of recognition. With something of chivalric devotedness in his manner he sunk on one knee before the duchess, and respectfully touched with his lips the hand she offered him. A gleam of eager anxiety darted into his eyes as he rose, looked at her, and saw the pining and joyless shadow which had settled on her divine features, her blanched delicacy of complexion.

'Your grace is wasting away,' said he abruptly, the first greeting being past. 'You are going into a decline; you have imagined things to be worse than they really are; you have frightened yourself with fantastic surmises.'

[Despite his desire to console her, Warner does not bring the longed-for letter. In desperation, Mary resolved to return with him to the front.]

'I cannot try one effort to soften him, separated by one hundred and twenty miles. He would think of me more as a woman, I am sure, and less as a bodiless link between himself and my terrible father if I were near at hand. Warner, this irritation throughout all my nerves is unbearable. I am not accustomed to disappointment and delay in what I wish. When do you return to Angria?'

'Tomorrow, my lady, before daylight, if possible.'

'And you travel incognito, of course?'

'I do.'

'Make room in your carriage then for me. I must go with you. Not a word, I implore you, Mr Warner, of expostulation. I should have died before morning if I had not hit upon this expedient.' Mr Warner heard her in silence and saw it was utterly vain to oppose her, but in his heart he hated the adventure. He saw its rashness and peril; besides he had calculated the result of the duke's determination over and over again. He had weighed advantages against disadvantages, profit against loss, the separation from the father against the happiness of the daughter, and in his serene and ambitious eye, the latter scale seemed far to kick the beam. He bowed to the duchess, said she should be obeyed, and left the room.

[Upon their arrival at the front Warner immediately meets with Zamorna.]

'I knew you were come, Howard,' said he, 'for I heard you voice below a quarter of an hour since. Well, have you procured the documents?'

'Yes, and I have delivered them to your grace's private secretary.'

'They were at Wellesley house, of course?'

'Yes, in the duchess's own keeping. She said you wished them to be preserved with care.

'Her grace,' continued Warner after a brief pause, 'asked very anxiously after you.'

The stern field-marshal look came over the duke, as he lay giantlike on his couch, and the momentary mildness melted away.

'I need not ask you how Mary Wellesley looks,' said he in his deep undertone, 'because I know better than you can tell me. I say, Howard, did she not ask you for a letter?'

'She did; she almost entreated me for one.'

'And you had not one to give her,' answered his sovereign, while with a low bitter laugh he turned on his couch and was silent.

Warner paced the room with a troubled step. 'My lord, are you doing right?' exclaimed he, pausing suddenly. 'The matter lies between God and your conscience. I know that the kingdom must be saved at any hazard of individual peace or even life; I advocate expediency, my lord, in the government of a state; I allow of equivocal measures to procure a just end; I sanction the shedding of blood and the cutting up of domestic happiness by the roots to stab a traitor to the heart.

But nevertheless I am a man, sire, and after what I have seen during the last day or two, I ask your majesty with solemn earnestness: is there no way by which the heart of Northangerland may be reached except through the breast of my queen?'

[Zamorna remains obdurate, and Warner finally quits him, with the intelligence that there is 'a lady' in the next room who wishes an audience with him.]

About ten minutes after Warner's departure, the lady in question entered the room by an inner door. Zamorna was now risen from his couch and stood in full stature before the fire. He turned to her at first carelessly, but his keen eye was quickly lit up with interest when he saw the elegant figure, whose slight, youthful proportions and graceful carriage, agreeing with her dress, produced an effect of such ladylike harmony. While dropping a profound obeisance, she contrived so to arrange her large veil as to hide her face. As she did this, her hand trembled; then she paused and leaned against a bookcase near the door.

Zamorna now saw that she shook from head to foot. Speaking in his tone of most soothing melody, he told her to draw near, and placed a chair for her close by the hearth. She made an effort to obey but it was evident she would have dropped if she had quitted her support. His grace smiled, a little surprised at her extreme agitation.

'I hope, madam,' said he, 'my presence is not the cause of your alarm,' and advancing, he kindly gave her his hand and led her to a seat. As she grew a little calmer he addressed her again in tones of the softest encouragement.

'I think Mr Warner said you are the wife of an officer in my army. What is his name?'

'Archer,' replied the lady, dropping one silver word for the first time.

'And have you any request to make concerning your husband? Speak our freely, madam; if it be reasonable, I will grant it.' She made some answer, but in a tone too low to be audible.

'Be so kind as to remove your veil, madam,' said the duke. 'It prevents me from hearing what you say distinctly.' She hesitated a moment, then as if she had formed some sudden resolution, she loosened the satin knot that confined her bonnet, and taking off both it and her veil, let them drop on the carpet. His majesty now caught a glimpse of a beautiful blushing face, but in a moment clusters of curls fell over it, and it was likewise concealed by two delicate little white hands with many rings sparkling on the taper fingers.

The sovereign of the east was nonplussed; he had an acute eye for most of these matters, but he did not quite understand the growing, trembling embarrassment of his lovely suppliant. He repeated the question he had before put to the lady respecting the nature of her petition.

'Sire,' said she at length, 'I want your majesty's gracious permission to see my dear, dear husband once more in this world before he leaves me forever.' She looked up, parted from her fair forehead her auburn curls, and raised her wild brown eyes, tearful and earnest and imploring, to a face that grew crimson under their glance.

The king's heart beat and throbbed till its motion could be seen in the heaving of a splendid chest. He seemed fixed in his attitude, standing before the lady, slightly bent over her, an inexpressible sparkle commencing and spreading to a flash in his eyes, the current of his lifeblood rising to his cheek, and his forehead dark with solemn, awful, desperate thought.

Mary clasped her hands and waited. She did not know whether love or indignation would prevail. She saw that both feelings were at work. Her suspense was at and end: the thundercloud broke asunder in a burst of electric passion! He turned from his duchess and flung open the door. A voice rung along the halls of Angria House summoning Warner—a voice having the spirit of a trumpet, the depth of a drum in its tone—

[Warner is duly rebuked in true imperial style, and dismissed.]

Warner, whose angelic philosophy had been little shaken by this appalling hurricane, would have stopped to give his grace a brief homily on the wickedness of indulging in violent passions; but a glance of entreaty from the duchess prevailed on him to withdraw in silence.

It was with a sensation of pleasurable terror that Mary found herself again alone with the duke. He had not yet spoken one harsh word to her. It was awful to be Zamorna's sole companion in this hour of his ire but how much better than to be one hundred and twenty miles away from him. She was soon near enough. The duke, gazing at her pale and sweet loveliness till he felt there was nothing in the world he loved half so well—conscious that her delicate attenuation was for his sake, appreciating too the idolatry that had brought her through such perils to see him at all hazards—threw himself impetuously beside her and soon made her tremble as much with the ardour of his caresses as she had done with the dread of his wrath.

'I'll seize the few hours of happiness you have thrown in my way, Mary,' said he, as she clung to him and called him her adored glorious Adrian, 'but these kisses and tears of thine, and this intoxicating beauty, shall not change my resolution. I *will* rend you, my lovely rose, entirely from me; I'll plant you in your father's garden again: I must do it, he compels me.'

'I don't care,' said the duchess, swallowing the delicious draught of the moment, and turning from the dark future to the glorious present shrined in Zamorna. 'But if you do divorce me, Zamorna, will you never, never take me back to you? Must I die inevitably before I am twenty?' The duke looked at her in silence; he could not cut off hope.

'The event has not taken place yet, Mary, and there lingers a possibility that it may be averted. But, love, should I take the crown off that sweet brow, the crown I placed over those silken curls on the day of our coronation, do not live hopeless. You may on some moonlight night hear Adrian's whistle under your window when you least expect it. Then step out on to the parapet; I'll lift you in my arms from thence to the terrace. From that time for ever, Mary, though Angria shall have no queen, a Percy shall have no daughter.'

'Adrian,' said the duchess, 'how different you are, how very different when I get close to you. At a distance you appear quite unapproachable. I wish, I wish my father was as near to you now as I am—or at least almost as near; because I am your creeping plant, I twine about you like ivy, and he is a tree to grow side by side with you. If he were in this room I should be satisfied.'

What answer Zamorna made I know not, but he brought down the curtain.

[An interval ensues; Zamorna is ultimately victorious and the rebellion put down; he is reconciled with Northangerland, against the vigorous objections of his advisors, and Mary is saved from the death which could surely have followed a permanent separation from her 'Adrian'. However, we next see Zamorna trying to extricate himself once again from his tenacious 'creeping plant'. He has bid good-bye to his family and is about to set off for Angria.]

The barouche stood at the door, the groom and the valet were waiting, and the duke, with a clouded countenance, was proceeding to join them, when his wife came forwards.

'You have forgotten me, Adrian—' she said in a very quiet tone, but her eye meantime flashed expressively. He started, for in truth he had forgotten her.

'Good-bye then, Mary,' he said, giving her a hurried kiss and embrace. She detained his hand.

'Pray, how long am I to stay here?' she asked. 'Why do you leave me at all? Why am I not to go with you?'

'It is such weather,' he answered. 'When this storm passes over I will send for you—'

'When will that be?' pursued the duchess, following his steps as he strode into the hall.

'Soon—soon my love—perhaps in a day or two—there now—don't be unreasonable—of course you cannot go today—'

'I can and I will,' answered the duchess quickly. 'I

have had enough of Alnwick, you shall not leave me behind you.'

'Go into the room, Mary. The door is open and the wind blows on you far too keenly. Don't you see how it drifts the snow in—'

"I will not go into the room. I'll step into the carriage as I am. If you refuse to wait till I can prepare, perhaps you will be humane enough to let me have a share of your cloak—' She shivered as she spoke. Her hair and her dress floated in the cold blast that blew in through the open entrance, strewing the hall with snow and dead leaves.

'You might wait till it is milder. I don't think it will do your grace any good to be out today—'

'But I must go, Mary—The Christmas recess is over and business presses.'

'Then do take me; I am sure I can bear it.'

'Out of the question. You may well clasp those small, silly hands—so thin I can almost see through them; and you may shake your curls over your face—to hide its paleness from me, I suppose. What is the matter? Crying? Good! What the devil am I do to with her? Go to your father, Mary. He has spoilt you.'

'Adrian, I cannot live at Alnwick without you,' said

26

the duchess earnestly, 'It recalls too forcibly the very bitterest days of my life. I'll not be separated from you again except by violence—'

The task of persuasion was no very easy one, for his own false play, his alienations, and his unnumbered treacheries had filled her mind with hideous phantoms of jealousy, had weakened her nerves and made them a prey to a hundred vague apprehensions; fears that never wholly left her except when she was actually in his arms or at least in his immediate presence.

'I tell you, Mary,' he said, regarding her with a smile half expressive of fondness—half of vexation—'I tell you I will send for you in two or three days—. Probably I shall be a week in Angria, not more—'

'A week! and your grace considers that but a short time? To me it will be most wearisome—'

'The horses will be frozen if they stand much longer,' returned the duke, not heeding her last remark. 'Come, wipe your eyes and be a little philosopher for once. There, let me have one smile before I go. A week will be over directly—this is not like setting out for a campaign.'

'Don't forget to send for me in two days,' pleaded the duchess as Zamorna released her from his arms.

'No, no, I'll send for you tomorrow—if the weather is settled enough. And,' half mimicking her voice, 'don't be jealous of me, Mary—unless you're afraid of the superior charms of Enara and Warner. Goodbye—' He was gone. She hurried to the window; he passed it. In three minutes the barouche swept with muffled sound round the lawn, shot down the carriage road, and was quickly lost in the thickening whirl of the snow storm.

[Mina, in the meantime, waits patiently for Zamorna at Rivaulx. As it happens, Lord Hartford is desperately in love with Mina; outraged by Zamorna's careless treatment of her, he decides to visit her and propose. He makes several attempts to broach the subject, but Mina pointedly avoids taking his meaning. Finally, however, his ardour becomes unmistakeable.]

Miss Laury agitatedly rose; she approached Hartford.

'My lord, you have been very kind to me, and I feel very grateful for that kindness. Perhaps sometime I may be able to repay it—we know not how the chances of fortune may turn; the weak have aided the

28

strong. I will watch vigilantly for the slightest opportunity to serve you, but do not talk in this way. I scarcely know whither your words tend.' Lord Hartford paused a moment before he replied. Gazing at her with bended brows and folded arms, he said,

'Miss Laury, what do you think of me?'

'That you are one of the noblest hearts in the world,' she replied unhesitatingly. She was standing just before Hartford, looking up at him, her hair falling back from her brow, shading with exquisite curls her temples and her slender neck. Her small sweet features, with that high seriousness deepening their beauty, were lit up by eyes so large, so dark, so swimming, so full of pleading benignity: an expression of alarmed regard, as if she at once feared for, and pitied, the sinful abstraction of a great mind.

Hartford could not stand it. He could have borne female anger or terror, but the look of enthusiastic gratitude, softened by compassion, nearly unmanned him. He turned his head for a moment aside, but then passion prevailed. Her beauty when he looked again struck through him a maddening sensation, whetted to acute power by a feeling like despair.

'You shall love me!' he exclaimed desperately. 'Do I

not love you? Would I not die for you? Must I in return receive only the cold regard of friendship? I am no platonist, Miss Laury—I am not your friend. I am, hear me, madam, your declared lover. Nay, you shall not leave me, by heaven! I am stronger than you are—' She had stepped a pace or two back, appalled by his vehemence. He thought she meant to withdraw; determined not to be so balked, he clasped her at once in both his arms and kissed her furiously rather than fondly. Miss Laury did not struggle.

'Hartford,' said she, steadying her voice, though it faltered in spite of her effort, 'this must be our parting scene. I will never see you again if you do not restrain yourself.' Hartford saw that she turned pale and he felt her tremble violently. His arms relaxed their hold. He allowed her to leave him. She sat down on a chair opposite and hurriedly wiped her brow, which was damp and marble-pale.

'Now, Miss Laury,' said his lordship, 'no man in the world loves you as I do. Will you accept my title and my coronet? I fling them at your feet.'

'My lord, do you know whose I am?' she replied in a hollow, very suppressed tone. 'Do you know with what a sound those proposals fall on my ear, how im-

pious and blasphemous they seem to be? Do you at all
conceive how utterly impossible it is that I should ever
love you? I thought you a true-hearted faithful man; I
find that you are a traitor.'

'And do you despise me?' asked Hartford.

'No, my lord, I do not.' She paused and looked
down. The colour rose rapidly into her pale face; she
sobbed, not in tears, but in the overmastering approach of an impulse born of a warm heart. Again she
looked up. Her eyes had changed, their aspect burning
with a wild bright inspiration.

'Hartford,' said she, 'had I met you long since, before I left home and dishonoured my father, I would
have loved you. O, my lord, you know not how truly.
I would have married you and made it the glory of my
life to cheer and brighten your hearth. But I cannot do
so now—never.

'I saw my present master when he had scarcely attained manhood. Do you think, Hartford, I will tell
you what feelings I had for him? No tongue could ex-
press them: they were so fervid, so glowing in their colour, that they effaced everything else. I lost the power
of properly appreciating the value of the world's opin-
ion, of discerning the difference between right and

31

wrong. I have never in my life contradicted Zamorna, never delayed obedience to his commands. I could not! He was sometimes more to me than a human being, he superseded all things: all affections, all interests, all fears or hopes or principles. Unconnected with him, my mind would be a blank—cold, dead, susceptible only of a sense of despair. How I should sicken if I were torn from him and thrown to you! Do not ask it—I would die first. No woman that ever loved my master could consent to leave him. There is nothing like him elsewhere. Hartford, if I were to be your wife, if Zamorna only looked at me, I should creep back like a slave to my former service. I should disgrace you as I have long since disgraced all my kindred. Think of that, my lord, and never say you love me again—'

[Hartford, stung to recklessness, finally insults Mina by a sarcastic reference to her as Zamorna's 'gentle mistress' whom he visits when he is tired by 'the turmoil of business and the teasing of matrimony'. They part abruptly, in bitterness.

More desperate than ever, Hartford challenges Zamorna to a duel; furious that 'a coarse Angrian squire' should seek to 'possess anything that had ever been mine', the duke inflicts a near-fatal wound on his rival.

Having dismissed Hartford, and unaware of the ensuing duel, Mina returns to her daily tasks, and to waiting for the duke. Mary, less patent than Mina, can wait no longer, and sets out for Zamorna's country house. An accident with her carriage lands her instead at Mina's Cross of Rivaulx, which is on the grounds of the duke's estate.]

Miss Laury was sitting after breakfast in a small library. Her desk lay before her, and two large ruled quartos filled with items and figures which she seemed to be comparing. Behind her chair stood a tall, well-made, soldierly, young man with light hair. His dress was plain and gentlemanly; the epaulette on one shoulder alone indicated an official capacity. He watched with a fixed look of attention the movements of the small fingers, which ascended in rapid calculation of long columns of accounts. It was strange to see the absorption of mind expressed in Miss Laury's face; the gravity of her smooth, white brow, shaded with drooping curls; the scarcely perceptible and unsmiling movement of her lips—though those lips in their rosy sweetness seemed formed only for smiles. An hour or more lapsed in the employment, the room meantime continuing in profound silence broken only by an occasional observation addressed by Miss Laury to the gentleman behind her concerning the legitimacy of some items, or the absence of some stray farthing, wanted to complete the necessary of the sum total. In the balancing of the books she displayed a most businesslike sharpness and strictness. The slightest fault was detected and remarked on in few words, but with a quick searching glance. However, the accountant had evidently been accustomed to her surveillance, for on the whole his books were a specimen of mathematical correctness.

'Very well,' said Miss Laury, as she closed the volumes. 'Your accounts do you credit, Mr O'Neill. You may tell his grace that all is quite right. Your memoranda tally with my own exactly.' Mr O'Neill bowed.

'Thank you, madam.' Taking up his books, he seemed about to leave the room. Before he did so, however, he turned and said,

'The duke wished me to inform you, madam, that he would probably be here about four or five o'clock in the afternoon.'

'Today?' asked Miss Laury in an accent of surprise.

'Yes, madam.' She paused a moment, then said quickly,

'Very well, sir.' Mr O'Neill now took his leave with another bow of low and respectful obeisance. Miss Laury returned it with a slight abstracted bow; her thoughts were all caught up and hurried away by that last communication. For a long time after the door had closed, she sat with her head on her hand, lost in a tumultuous flush of ideas—anticipations awakened by that simple sentence, 'The duke will be here today.'

The striking of the timepiece roused her. She remembered that twenty tasks waited her direction. Always active, always employed, it was not her custom to while away hours in dreaming. She rose, closed her desk, and left the quiet library for busier scenes.

Four o'clock came and Miss Laury's foot was heard on the staircase, descending from her chamber. She crossed the large, light passage, an apparition of feminine elegance and beauty. She had dressed herself splendidly: the robe of black satin became at once her slender form, which it enveloped in full and shining folds, and her bright, blooming complexion, which it set off by the contrast of colour. Glittering through her curls there was a band of fine diamonds, and drops of the same pure gem trembled from her small, delicate ears. These ornaments, so regal in their nature, had been the gift of royalty, and were worn now chiefly for the associations of soft and happy moments which their gleam might be supposed to convey.

She entered her drawing room and stood by the window. From thence appeared one glimpse of the high-road, visible through the thickening shades of Rivaulx; even that was now almost concealed by the frozen mist in which the approach of twilight was wrapt. All was very quiet, both in the house and in the wood. A carriage drew near, she heard the sound. She saw it shoot through the fog. But it was not Zamorna.

She had not gazed a minute before her experienced eye discerned that there was something wrong with the horses—the harness had got entangled, or they were frightened. The coachman had lost command over them, they were plunging violently. She rung the bell; a servant entered; she ordered immediate assistance to be despatched to that carriage on the road. Two grooms presently hurried down the drive to execute her commands, but before they could reach the spot, one of the horses, in its gambols, had slipped on the icy road and fallen. The others grew more unmanageable, and presently the carriage lay overturned on the roadside. One of Miss Laury's messengers came back. She threw up the window.

'Anybody hurt?'

'I hope not much, madam.'

'Who is in the carriage?'

'Only one lady, and she seems to have fainted. She looked very white when I opened the door. What is to be done, madam?' Miss Laury, with Irish frankness, answered directly.

'Bring the lady in directly, and make the servants comfortable.'

'Yes, madam.'

Miss Laury shut her window; it was very cold. Not many minutes elapsed before the lady, in the arms of her own servant, was slowly brought up the lawn and ushered into the drawing-room.

'Lay her on the sofa,' said Miss Laury. The lady's travelling cloak was carefully removed, and a thin figure became apparent in a dark silk dress: the cushions of down scarcely sunk under the pressure, it was so light.

Her swoon was now passing off. The genial warmth

of the fire, which shone full on her, revived her. Opening her eyes, she looked up at Miss Laury's face, who was bending close over her, wetting her lips with some cordial. Recognising a stranger, she shyly turned her glance aside. She looked keenly round the room, and seeing the perfect elegance of its arrangement, the cheerful and tranquil glow of a hearthlight, she appeared to grow more composed.

'To whom am I indebted for this kindness? Where am I?'

'In a hospitable country, madam. The Angrians never turn their backs on strangers.'

'I know I am in Angria,' she said quietly, 'but where? What is the name of this house, and who are you?'

Miss Laury coloured slightly. It seemed as if there were some undefinable reluctance to give her real name; she knew she was widely celebrated—too widely; most likely the lady would turn from her in contempt if she heard it. Miss Laury felt she could not bear that.

'I am only the housekeeper,' she said. 'This is a shooting lodge belonging to a great Angrian proprietor—'

'Who?' asked the lady, who was not to be put off by indirect answers. Again Miss Laury hesitated; for her life she could not have said 'His Grace the Duke of Zamorna.' She replied hastily.

'A gentleman of western extraction, a distant branch of the great Pakenhams—so at least the family records say, but they have been long naturalised in the east—'

'I never heard of them,' replied the lady. 'Pakenham? That is not an Angrian name!'

'Perhaps, madam, you are not particularly acquainted with this part of the country—'

'I know Hawkscliffe,' said the lady, 'and your house is on the very borders, within the royal liberties, is it not?'

'Yes, madam. It stood there before the great duke bought up the forest manor, and his majesty allowed my master to retain this lodge and the privilege of sporting in the chase.'

'Well, and you are Mr Pakenham's housekeeper?'

'Yes, madam.' The lady surveyed Miss Laury with another furtive side-glance of her large, majestic eyes. Those eyes lingered upon the diamond earrings, the bandeau of brilliants that flashed from between the clusters of raven curls; then passed over the sweet face, the exquisite figure of the young housekeeper; and finally were reverted to the wall with an expression that spoke volumes. Miss Laury could have torn the dazzling pendants from her ears; she was bitterly stung.

'Everybody knows me,' she said to herself. ' "Mistress" I suppose is branded on my brow—'

[Realizing that Mina is lying, Mary asks for a room to withdraw to and concocts her own story: she is 'Mrs Irving', whose husband is a minister from the north. Mary retires; Mina, below, awaits Zamorna's arrival.]

Five o'clock now struck. It was nearly dark. A servant with a taper was lighting up the chandeliers in the large dining room where a table, spread for dinner, received the kindling lamplight upon a starry service of silver. It was likewise flashed back from a splendid sideboard, all arranged in readiness to receive the great, the expected, guest.

Tolerably punctual in keeping an appointment—when he meant to keep it at all—Zamorna entered the house as the fairylike voice of a musical clock in the passage struck out its symphony to the pendulum. The opening of the front door, a bitter rush of the night wind; then the sudden close and the step advancing were the signals of his arrival.

Miss Laury was in the dining room looking round and giving the last touch to all things. She just met her master as he entered. His cold lip pressed to her forehead, and his colder hand clasping hers, brought the sensation which it was her custom of weeks and months to wait for, and to consider, when attained, as the single recompense of all delay and all toil, all suffering.

'I am frozen, Mina,' said he. 'I came on horseback for the last four miles and the night is like Canada.' Chafing his icy hand to animation between her own warm and supple palms, she answered by the speechless but expressive look of joy, satisfaction, and idolatry which filled and overflowed her eyes.

'What can I do for you, my lord?' were her first words, as he stood by the fire raising his hands cheerily over the blaze. He laughed.

'Put your arms around my neck, Mina, and kiss my cheek as warm and blooming as your own.'

If Mina Laury had been Mina Wellesley, she would have done so; and it gave her a pang to resist the impulse that urged her to take him at his word. But she put it by and only diffidently drew near the arm chair into which he had now thrown himself, and began to smooth and separate the curls on his temples. She noticed, as the first smile of salutation subsided, a gloom succeeded on her master's brow, which, however he spoke or laughed afterwards, remained a settled characteristic of his countenance.

'What visitors are in the house?' he asked. 'I saw the groom rubbing down four black horses before the stables as I came in.'

'A carriage was overturned at the lodge gates about an hour since; as the lady who was in it was taken out insensible, I ordered her to be brought up here and her servants accommodated for the night.'

'And do you know who the lady is?' continued his grace. 'The horses are good—first rate.'

'She says her name is Mrs Irving, and that she is the wife of a Presbyterian minister in the north, but—'

'You hardly believe her?' interrupted the duke.

'No,' returned Miss Laury. 'I must say I took her for a lady of rank. She has something highly aristocratic about her manners and aspect, and she appeared to know a good deal about Angria.'

'What is she like?' asked Zamorna. 'Young or old, handsome or ugly?'

'She is young, slender, not so tall as I, and I should

say rather elegant than handsome; very pale and cold in her demeanour. She has a small mouth and chin and a very fair neck—'

'Perhaps you did not say to whom the house belonged, Mina?'

'I said,' replied Mina smiling, 'the owner of the house was a great Angrian proprietor, a lineal descendant of the western Pakenhams, and that I was his housekeeper.'

'Very good; she would not believe you. You look like an Angrian country gentleman's dolly. Give me your hand, my girl. Are you not as old as I am?'

'Yes, my lord duke. I was born on the same day, an hour after your grace.'

'So I have heard, but it must be a mistake. You don't look twenty, and I am twenty-five, my beautiful western. What eyes! Look at me, Mina—straight and don't blush—' Mina tried to look, but she could not do it without blushing. She coloured to the temples.

'Pshaw!' said his grace, putting her away. 'Pretending to be modest. My acquaintance of ten years cannot meet my eye unshrinkingly. Have you lost that ring I once gave you, Mina?'

'What ring, my lord? You have given me many.'

'That which I said had the essence of your whole heart and mind engraven in the stone as a motto.'

'Fidelity?' asked Miss Laury, and she held out her hand with a graven emerald on her forefinger.

'Right,' was the reply. 'Is it your motto still?' And with one of his haughty, jealous glances he seemed trying to read her conscience. Miss Laury at once saw that late transactions were not a secret confined between herself and Lord Hartford. She saw his grace was unhinged and strongly inclined to be savage; she stood and watched him with a sad, fearful gaze.

'Well,' she said, turning away after a long pause, 'If your grace is angry with me, I've very little to care about in this world—' The entrance of servants with the dinner prevented Zamorna's answer . . .

It was not till after the cloth was withdrawn and the servants had retired that the duke, whilst he sipped his single glass of champagne, recommenced the conversation he had before so unpleasantly entered upon.

'Come here, my girl,' he said, drawing a seat close to his side. Mina never delayed nor hesitated, through bashfulness or any other feeling, to comply with his orders.

'Now,' he continued, leaning his head towards hers, and placing his hand on her shoulder, 'are you happy, Mina? Do you want anything?'

'Nothing, my lord.' She spoke truly. All that was capable of yielding her happiness on this side of eternity was at that moment within her reach. The room was full of calm. The lamps hung as if they were listening; the fire sent up no flickering flame, but diffused a broad, still, glowing light over all the spacious saloon. Zamorna touched her. His form and features filled her eye, his voice her ear, his presence her whole heart. She was soothed to perfect happiness.

'My Fidelity,' pursued that musical voice, 'if thou hast any favour to ask, now is the time. I'm all concession—as sweet as honey, as yielding as a lady's glove. Come, Esther, what is thy petition and thy request? Even to the half of my kingdom it shall be granted.'

'Nothing', again murmured Miss Laury. 'Oh, my lord, nothing. What can I want?'

'Nothing?' he repeated. 'What, no reward for ten years' faith and love and devotion? No reward for the companionship in six months' exile? No recompense to the little hand that has so often smoothed my pillow in sickness, to the sweet lips that have many a time in cool and dewy health been pressed to a brow of fever? None to the dark Milesian eyes that once grew dim with watching through endless nights by my couch of delirium? Need I speak of the sweetness and fortitude that cheered sufferings known only to thee and me, Mina, of the devotion that gave me bread when thou wert dying of hunger, and that scarcely more than a year since? For all this and much more must there be no reward?'

'I have had it,' said Miss Laury, 'I have it now—'

'But,' continued the duke, 'what if I have devised something worthy of your acceptance? Look up now and listen to me.' She did look up, but she speedily looked down again. Her master's eye was insupportable; it burnt absolutely with infernal fire.

'What is he going to say?' murmured Miss Laury to herself. She trembled.

'I say, love,' pursued the individual, drawing her a little closer to him, 'I will give you as a reward a husband—don't start now—and that husband shall be a nobleman, and that nobleman is called Lord Hartford! Now, madam, stand up and let me look at you.'

He opened his arms and Miss Laury sprang erect like a loosened bow.

'Your grace is anticipated!' she said. 'That offer has been made me before. Lord Hartford did it himself three days ago.'

'And what did you say, madam? Speak the truth now. Subterfuge won't avail you—'

'What did I say? Zamorna, I don't know—it little signifies. You have rewarded me, my lord duke, but I cannot bear this. I feel sick.' With a deep short sob, she turned white, and fell, close by the duke, her head against his foot.

This was the first time in her life that Miss Laury had fainted, but strong health availed nothing against the deadly struggle which convulsed every feeling of her nature when she heard her master's announcement. She believed him to be perfectly sincere; she thought he was tired of her and she could not stand it.

I suppose Zamorna's first feeling when she fell was horror; and his next, I am tolerably certain, was intense gratification. People say I am not in earnest when I abuse him, or else I would here insert half a page of deserved vituperation: deserved and heartfelt. As it is, I will merely relate his conduct, without note or comment. He took a wax taper from the table and held it over Miss Laury. Hers could be no dissimulation: she went white as marble and still as stone. In truth, then, she did intensely love him with a devotion that left no room in her thoughts for one shadow of an alien image. Do not think, reader, that Zamorna meant to be so generous as to bestow Miss Laury on Lord Hartford. No; trust him; he was but testing in his usual way the attachment which a thousand proofs daily given ought long ago to have convinced him was undying.

While he yet gazed, she began to recover. Her eyelids stirred; then slowly dawned from beneath the large black orbs that scarcely met his before they filled to overflowing with sorrow. Not a gleam of anger, not a whisper of reproach; her lips and eyes spoke together no other language than the simple words,

'I cannot leave you.' She rose feebly, and with effort. The duke stretched out his hand to assist her. He held to her lips the scarcely tasted wine glass. 'Mina,' he said, 'are you collected enough to hear me?'

'Yes, my lord.'

'Then listen. I would much sooner give half—aye, the whole of my estates to Lord Hartford than yourself. What I said just now was only to try you.' Miss

Laury raised her eyes, sighed like awaking from some hideous dream, but she could not speak.

"Would I,' continued the duke, 'would I resign the possession of my first love to any hands but my own? I would far rather see her in her coffin. I would lay you there as still, as white, and much more lifeless than you were stretched just now at my feet, before I would for threat, for entreaty, for purchase, give to another a glance of your eye, a smile from your lip. I know you adore me now, for you could not feign that agitation; and therefore I will tell you what a proof I gave yesterday of my regard for you. Hartford mentioned your name in my presence, and I revenged the profanation by a shot which sent him to his bed little better than a corpse.'

Miss Laury shuddered, but so dark and profound are the mysteries of human nature, ever allying vice with virtue, that I fear this bloody proof of her master's love brought to her heart more rapture than horror. She said not a word, for now Zamorna's arms were again folded round her; again he was soothing her to tranquillity, by endearments and caresses that far away removed all thought of the world, all past pangs of shame, all cold doubts, all weariness, all heartsickness resulting from hope long-deferred. He had told her that she was his first love, and now she felt tempted to believe that she was likewise his only love. Strong-minded beyond her sex, active, energetic, and accomplished in all other points of view, here she was as weak as a child. She lost her identity. Her very way of life was swallowed up in that of another.

[The tête-à-tête is interrupted by Zamorna's valet, who calls him from the room to deliver the embarrassing intelligence that 'Mrs Irving', now wandering about the halls, bears a disconcerting resemblance to his wife, the duchess.]

'I was walking carelessly through the passage about ten minutes since, when I heard a step on the stairs—a light step, as if of a very small foot. I turned, and there was a lady coming down. My lord, she was a lady!'

'Well, sir, did you know her?'

'I think, if my eyes were not bewitched, I did. I stood in the shade screened by a pillar and she passed very near without observing me. I saw her distinctly, and may I be damned this very moment if it was not—'

'Who, sir?'

'The duchess!!' There was a pause, which was closed by a remarkably prolonged whistle from the duke. He put both his hands into his pockets and took a leisurely turn through the room. 'You're sure?' he said. 'I know you dare not tell me a lie in such matters. Aye, it's true enough, I'll be sworn. Mrs Irving, wife of a minister in the north. A satirical hit at my royal self, by God. Pale, fair neck, little mouth and chin. Very good! I wish that same little mouth and chin were about a hundred miles off. What can have brought her? Anxiety about her invaluable husband? Could not bear any longer without him? Obliged to set off to see what he was doing? If she had entered the room unexpectedly about five minutes since—God! I should have had no resource but to tie her hand and foot. It would have killed her. What the devil shall I do? Must not be angry, she can't do with that sort of thing just now. Talk softly, reprove her gently, swear black and white to my having no connection with Mr Pakenham's housekeeper—' Closing his sililoquy, the duke turned again to his valet.

'What room did her grace go into?'

'The drawing room, my lord. She's there now.'

'Well, say nothing about it, on pain of sudden death.

Do you hear sir?' He laid his hand on his heart and Zamorna left the room to commence operations.

Softly unclosing the drawing room door, he perceived a lady by the hearth. Her back was towards him, but there could be no mistake. The whole turn of form, the style of dress, the curled auburn head: all were attributes of but one person, of his own unique, haughty, jealous little duchess. He closed the door as noiselessly as he had opened it, and stole forwards.

The duchess felt a hand press her shoulder, and she looked up. The force of attraction had its usual result, and she clung to what she saw.

'Adrian! Adrian!' was all her lips could utter.

'Mary! Mary!' replied the duke, allowing her to hang about him. 'Pretty doings! What brought you here? Are you running away, eloping in my absence?'

'Adrian, why did you leave me? You said you would come back in a week, and it's eight days since you left me. Do come home—'

'So, you actually have set off in search of a husband,' said Zamorna, laughing heartily, 'and been overturned and obliged to take shelter in Pakenham's shooting box!'

'Why are you here, Adrian?' enquired the duchess,

who was far too much in earnest to join in his laugh. 'Who is Pakenham and who is that person who calls herself his housekeeper? Why do you let anybody live so near Hawkscliffe without ever telling me?'

'I forgot to tell you,' said his grace. 'I've other things to think about when those bright hazel eyes are looking up at me. As for Pakenham, to tell you the truth—he's a sort of left-hand cousin of your own, being natural son to the old admiral, my uncle, in the south; his housekeeper is his sister. Voilà tout. Kiss me now.' The duchess did kiss him, but it was with a heavy sigh. The cloud of jealous anxiety hung on her brow undissipated.

'Adrian, my heart aches still. Why have you been staying so long in Angria? O, you don't care for me! You have never thought how miserably I have been longing for your return. Adrian—' she stopped and cried.

'Mary, recollect yourself,' said his grace. 'I cannot be always at your feet. You were not so weak when we were first married. You let me leave you often then without any jealous remonstrance.'

'I did not know you so well at that time,' said Mary, 'and if my mind is weakened, all its strength has gone away in tears and terrors for you. I am neither so handsome nor so cheerful as I once was. But you ought to forgive my decay because you have caused it.'

'Mary, never again reproach yourself with loss of beauty till I give the hint first. Believe me now, in that and every other respect, you are just what I wish you to be. You cannot fade any more than marble can—at least not to my eyes. As for your devotion and tenderness, though I chide its excess sometimes because it wastes and bleaches you almost to a shadow, yet it forms the very firmest chain that binds me to you. Now cheer up. Tonight you shall go to Hawkscliffe; it is only five miles off. I cannot accompany you because I have some important business to transact with Pakenham which must not be deferred. Tomorrow I will be at the castle before dawn. The carriage shall be ready, I will put you in, myself beside you. Off we go, straight to Verdopolis, and there for the next three months I will tire you of my company, morning, noon, and night. Now, what can I promise more? If you choose to be jealous, why, I can't help it. I must then take to soda water and despair, or have myself petrified and carved into an Apollo for your dressing room. Lord! I get no credit with my virtue—' By dint of lies and laughter the individual at last succeeded in getting all things settled to his mind. The duchess went to Hawkscliffe that night. Keeping his promise, for once, he accompanied her to Verdopolis the next morning—

Lord Hartford still lies between life and death. His passion is neither weakened by pain, piqued by rejection, nor cooled by absence. On the iron nerves of the man are graven an impression which nothing can efface.

For a long space of time, good-bye reader. I have done my best to please you, and though I know that through feebleness, dullness, and iteration my work terminates rather in failure than triumph, yet you are bound to forgive, for I have done my best—

January, 1838

PENGUIN 60s CLASSICS

APOLLONIUS OF RHODES · *Jason and the Argonauts*
ARISTOPHANES · *Lysistrata*
SAINT AUGUSTINE · *Confessions of a Sinner*
JANE AUSTEN · *The History of England*
HONORÉ DE BALZAC · *The Atheist's Mass*
BASHŌ · *Haiku*
GIOVANNI BOCCACCIO · *Ten Tales from the* Decameron
JAMES BOSWELL · *Meeting Dr Johnson*
CHARLOTTE BRONTË · *Mina Laury*
CAO XUEQIN · *The Dream of the Red Chamber*
THOMAS CARLYLE · *On Great Men*
BALDESAR CASTIGLIONE · *Etiquette for Renaissance Gentlemen*
CERVANTES · *The Jealous Extremaduran*
KATE CHOPIN · *The Kiss*
JOSEPH CONRAD · *The Secret Sharer*
DANTE · *The First Three Circles of Hell*
CHARLES DARWIN · *The Galapagos Islands*
THOMAS DE QUINCEY · *The Pleasures and Pains of Opium*
DANIEL DEFOE · *A Visitation of the Plague*
BERNAL DÍAZ · *The Betrayal of Montezuma*
FYODOR DOSTOYEVSKY · *The Gentle Spirit*
FREDERICK DOUGLASS · *The Education of Frederick Douglass*
GEORGE ELIOT · *The Lifted Veil*
GUSTAVE FLAUBERT · *A Simple Heart*
BENJAMIN FRANKLIN · *The Means and Manner of Obtaining Virtue*
EDWARD GIBBON · *Reflections on the Fall of Rome*
CHARLOTTE PERKINS GILMAN · *The Yellow Wallpaper*
GOETHE · *Letters from Italy*
HOMER · *The Rage of Achilles*
HOMER · *The Voyages of Odysseus*

PENGUIN 60S CLASSICS

HENRY JAMES · *The Lesson of the Master*
FRANZ KAFKA · *The Judgement*
THOMAS À KEMPIS · *Counsels on the Spiritual Life*
HEINRICH VON KLEIST · *The Marquise of O—*
LIVY · *Hannibal's Crossing of the Alps*
NICCOLÒ MACHIAVELLI · *The Art of War*
SIR THOMAS MALORY · *The Death of King Arthur*
GUY DE MAUPASSANT · *Boule de Suif*
FRIEDRICH NIETZSCHE · *Zarathustra's Discourses*
OVID · *Orpheus in the Underworld*
PLATO · *Phaedrus*
EDGAR ALLAN POE · *The Murders in the Rue Morgue*
ARTHUR RIMBAUD · *A Season in Hell*
JEAN-JACQUES ROUSSEAU · *Meditations of a Solitary Walker*
ROBERT LOUIS STEVENSON · *Dr Jekyll and Mr Hyde*
TACITUS · *Nero and the Burning of Rome*
HENRY DAVID THOREAU · *Civil Disobedience*
LEO TOLSTOY · *The Death of Ivan Ilyich*
IVAN TURGENEV · *Three Sketches from a Hunter's Album*
MARK TWAIN · *The Man That Corrupted Hadleyburg*
GIORGIO VASARI · *Lives of Three Renaissance Artists*
EDITH WHARTON · *Souls Belated*
WALT WHITMAN · *Song of Myself*
OSCAR WILDE · *The Portrait of Mr W. H.*

ANONYMOUS WORKS

Beowulf and Grendel
Gilgamesh and Enkidu
Tales of Cú Chulaind

Buddha's Teachings
Krishna's Dialogue on the Soul
Two Viking Romances

READ MORE IN PENGUIN

For complete information about books available from Penguin and how to order them, please write to us at the appropriate address below. Please note that for copyright reasons the selection of books varies from country to country.

IN THE UNITED KINGDOM: Please write to *Dept. EP, Penguin Books Ltd, Bath Road, Harmondsworth, Middlesex UB7 0DA.*

IN THE UNITED STATES: Please write to *Consumer Sales, Penguin USA, P.O. Box 999, Dept. 17109, Bergenfield, New Jersey 07621-0120.* VISA and MasterCard holders call 1-800-253-6476 to order Penguin titles.

IN CANADA: Please write to *Penguin Books Canada Ltd, 10 Alcorn Avenue, Suite 300, Toronto, Ontario M4V 3B2.*

IN AUSTRALIA: Please write to *Penguin Books Australia Ltd, P.O. Box 257, Ringwood, Victoria 3134.*

IN NEW ZEALAND: Please write to *Penguin Books (NZ) Ltd, Private Bag 102902, North Shore Mail Centre, Auckland 10.*

IN INDIA: Please write to *Penguin Books India Pvt Ltd, 706 Eros Apartments, 56 Nehru Place, New Delhi 110 019.*

IN THE NETHERLANDS: Please write to *Penguin Books Netherlands bv, Postbus 3507, NL-1001 AH Amsterdam.*

IN GERMANY: Please write to *Penguin Books Deutschland GmbH, Metzlerstrasse 26, 60594 Frankfurt am Main.*

IN SPAIN: Please write to *Penguin Books S. A., Bravo Murillo 19, 1º B, 28015 Madrid.*

IN ITALY: Please write to *Penguin Italia s.r.l., Via Felice Casati 20, I-20124 Milano.*

IN FRANCE: Please write to *Penguin France S. A., 17 rue Lejeune, F-31000 Toulouse.*

IN JAPAN: Please write to *Penguin Books Japan, Ishikiribashi Building, 2-5-4, Suido, Bunkyo-ku, Tokyo 112.*

IN GREECE: Please write to *Penguin Hellas Ltd, Dimocritou 3, GR-106 71 Athens.*

IN SOUTH AFRICA: Please write to *Longman Penguin Southern Africa (Pty) Ltd, Private Bag X08, Bertsham 2013.*